Rebekah – Girl Detective

Books 9 - 12

PJ Ryan

Cover Illustration by Carolina Storni

ISBN: 0615906443

ISBN-13: 978-0615906447

Contents

"Rebekah - Girl Detective" is a short story series for children ages 9-12 with the remaining titles to be published on a regular basis. Each title can be read on its own.

You can join Rebekah's fun Facebook page for young detectives here:

http://www.facebook.com/RebekahGirlDetective

I'd really love to hear from you!

I very much appreciate your reviews and comments so thank you in advance for taking a moment to leave one for "Rebekah - Girl Detective: Books 9-12."

Sincerely,

PJ

All Titles by PJ Ryan Can be Found Here (Author Page)
http://www.amazon.com/author/pjryan

Look for the following series with more coming soon!

Rebekah – Girl Detective

RJ – Boy Detective

Mouse's Secret Club

Rebekah – Girl Detective #9

Mystery At Summer Camp

Rebekah - Girl Detective #9

Mystery At Summer Camp

Chapter 1

Rebekah had been counting down the days until school ended. It was not because she didn't like school. She did. It was because as soon as the days started heating up and getting longer, she knew that summer was coming. Which meant summer camp. It also meant she would get to spend some time with her older cousin RJ.

"I can't wait, I can't wait," she said to Mouse as soon as school ended.

"Me either," Mouse grinned. He went to the same summer camp she did. "I wonder if they'll have that delicious bread pudding again."

"Ugh," Rebekah shook her head. "That's the only thing I don't like about summer camp."

"Well that's alright, you can give me yours," Mouse laughed.

On the morning they were to leave, Rebekah was so excited that she could barely stand waiting for the bus.

"I can't wait, I can't wait, I can't wait!" she whispered gleefully. Mouse rolled his eyes and sighed with relief when the bus finally arrived. The trip was a long one, taking them from the little town of Curtis Bay to the sprawling woods. When they climbed off of the bus, there were already many kids at the camp. They were all chatting loudly and greeting each other after a year apart. Rebekah waved to a few of the kids that she remembered from the year before, but she was really only looking for one very familiar face. That face was not hard to find, because the boy it belonged to was perched on a branch in a tall tree not far off from the group.

"RJ!" Rebekah shouted happily and waved to him. Mouse waved eagerly too and they both ran over to the older boy. RJ was eleven, which made him practically a grown up in Rebekah's mind. He was her cousin, and each year they went to the same summer camp together. RJ had taught her a lot about being a detective, because he was an official Junior Detective. He mailed away for a kit and everything. The year before he showed Rebekah the magnifying glass and fingerprinting set that had come in the kit. He even had his very own badge.

RJ had red hair, just like Rebekah, but he always wore a detective hat, even when he went swimming!

"Hi there!" RJ grinned as he jumped down from the tree branch to greet them. "I've been waiting for you guys all morning," he gave his cousin a quick hug and patted Mouse on the back. When he did, a little white mouse poked its nose up out of Mouse's pocket. It wiggled its whiskers at RJ.

"Aha, I see that you have brought one of your pets," RJ said nervously. He was not a big fan of mice.

"Don't worry," Mouse said with a grin. "This is Magellan. He's supposed to be a famous explorer, but really," he whispered his next words. "He's a scaredy-mouse!"

Mouse was right, because his little pet dove right back into his pocket the moment he saw all of the commotion around him.

"Are you ready for a great summer?" Rebekah asked cheerfully as she, RJ, and Mouse walked toward their cabins.

"It's great to be back in the fresh air," RJ said, and then lowered his voice. "And out of the dangers of the city."

"Dangers?" Mouse asked with a squeak.

"Oh yes," RJ nodded. "There have been many mysteries for me to solve this year."

"We've been solving mysteries too," Rebekah said proudly, and Mouse nodded.

"You must always be careful," RJ warned. "Detective work is best left to professionals," he showed her the badge he had clipped to his belt.

Rebekah nodded, but she felt a little sad. She knew she was a good detective and she wanted her cousin to know that too.

Chapter 2

Mouse and RJ were staying in a boys' cabin, while Rebekah was staying on the other side of the campfire, in a girls' cabin. She was sad to have to stay alone, but there were a few girls she knew from the year before and some nice new friends to make too. However, as soon as they had their things settled, RJ and Mouse came running over to her cabin.

"There's going to be a sing-a-long!" Mouse said happily.

RJ rolled his eyes. "Kid stuff."

Rebekah frowned. She loved the sing-a-long. Did that make her too much of a kid? As they gathered in the bleachers around the campfire, they were all chatting with one another. It wasn't until a few minutes passed that the campers began to realize that there was no one waiting to lead them with the singing. In fact, there were no counselors around at all. Then suddenly in the center of the campground there was a big burst of smoke. It seemed to come from nowhere!

"What was that?" Rebekah shouted as she stood up. RJ stood up right beside her and they both looked ready to investigate. But when the smoke cleared, the sound of a guitar filled their ears. Where no one had stood a moment before, was a man dressed in a counselor's outfit with a guitar slung over his shoulder.

He began to sing the camp song. All of the kids in the bleachers were so shocked by the scene that they didn't sing along. The man who had long blonde hair and brown eyes with a big smile continued to sing as if he didn't care if none of the students sung along.

Mouse, who was staring with wide eyes and an open mouth began to clap loudly. Soon the other kids began to clap too. Rebekah was the first one to start singing, then the other kids, except for RJ of course, joined in. When the song was over the counselor introduced himself.

"My name is Louis, and I am a new counselor here this year. I'll be in charge of entertainment. We'll be having lots of campfires, and even a play, and a magic show."

"A magic show!" Mouse squealed and could barely keep from jumping up and down on the bleachers. Mouse was a big fan of magic and was hoping to be a magician himself one day. "This year is going to be great!"

RJ sighed. "Great, singing, acting and magic. Where's the fun in that?"

"I think it'll be fun," Rebekah said firmly. "But I bet we don't get through the summer without stumbling over a mystery or two."

"I hope so," RJ grinned. "I have a lot to teach you little cousin."

Chapter 3

After the sing-a-long was over, the three began exploring the campground. There was not much new to see, as they had been attending the camp for a few years. But Rebekah found the bird's nest she had spotted the year before, and it had new baby birds in it. Mouse found the little cage he had made out of twines and branches for the last mouse pet he had brought along, right where he left it.

"Are you sure he can't get out of there?" RJ asked suspiciously as he peered into the cage.

"The last one didn't," Mouse shrugged.

RJ glanced up from the cage and noticed something glittering in the leaves ahead of them.

"What's that?" he wondered. When he stepped closer and brushed the leaves away he discovered that it was a sparkly guitar pick.

"Weird," Rebekah frowned. "What would a guitar pick be doing all the way out here?"

"Maybe someone dropped it on a hike," Mouse suggested.

"Maybe," Rebekah said thoughtfully. "We should bring it back to the camp and see if anyone lost it."

"Sure," RJ nodded, but he was staring at the pick. As they walked back to the camp the sun was setting. It was time to share a meal and then head back to their cabins for the night. At dinner they were treated to hamburgers and french fries, a celebration of their first night at camp. After dinner they told a few ghost stories around the campfire.

"That's not possible," RJ muttered to Rebekah when one of the kids told a story about a zombie.

"Maybe it wasn't really a zombie, but somebody dressed up like a zombie," Rebekah pointed out.

"Good thinking little cuz," RJ said with a grin. "You get smarter every time I see you."

Rebekah went back to her cabin with a grin on her face. She was so proud of the compliment her cousin had given her that she forgot entirely about the guitar pick they had found in the woods.

Chapter 4

Early the next morning Rebekah heard a knocking on the door of her cabin. Most of the other kids in her cabin were still sleeping. She walked sleepily to the door and found Mouse standing on the other side.

"Rebekah something terrible has happened!" he announced.

"What is it?" Rebekah asked with a gasp.

"Mr. Louis is gone!" he said in a whisper. "He's disappeared!"

Rebekah stepped outside of the cabin still in her pajamas and closed the door. She looked Mouse directly in the eyes.

"What do you mean he disappeared?"

Mouse sighed and started again. "I got up early this morning because I wanted to ask Mr. Louis if I could help him with his magic show. But when I knocked on the counselor's cabin, they said that Mr. Louis was gone."

"What do you mean gone?" Rebekah pressed with frustration.

"Well," Mouse hesitated. "They said he must have gone home, they hadn't seen him after the sing-a-long yesterday."

"Oh Mouse," Rebekah sighed. "Going home is not exactly the same thing as disappearing, is it?"

"No," he frowned. "But Rebekah I don't believe it. Didn't you see how excited he was yesterday about putting on all the shows? Why would he just decide to leave?"

Rebekah frowned too, it did seem strange. "Well maybe he had an emergency. Or maybe he realized how many mosquitoes are in the woods!" she smacked her arm sharply as a mosquito made a feast out of her.

"I don't think so," Mouse shook his head. "Rebekah, I know I'm not usually the one who finds the mysteries, but I have a feeling about this one."

"And what feeling would that be?" RJ asked from just behind them. He had woken up early to investigate some sounds he had heard the night before outside of his cabin.

"Mr. Louis is gone," Mouse explained quickly.

"Maybe the Bertha got him," another voice said. It was a kid even older than RJ. He was going to blow the bugle to wake everyone up for the morning when he overheard their conversation.

"Who's Bertha?" RJ asked.

"You've never heard of Bertha?" the boy asked with a chuckle. "She's the bear that lives in these woods."

"What?" Rebekah shook her head. "I've never heard of any bear living in these woods."

"Oh," the boy lowered his voice. "That's because you're just kids. They don't want to scare you. But my big brother was a counselor here, and he told me all about Bertha. She's a giant bear and every once in a while she gets hungry."

Rebekah shivered at the thought. Mouse glared at the boy and RJ tapped his chin thoughtfully.

"Well, if the bear were big enough," he shrugged.

"Mr. Louis did not get eaten by a bear!" Mouse said and stomped his foot against the dirt. "This kid is just trying to scare us. Aren't you?" he asked.

"Well," the older boy shrugged. "I guess until you see her for yourself, you'll never believe me!" with that he stalked off to the microphone that he would blow his bugle into.

"Do you think he might be right?" Rebekah asked quietly.

"No way," Mouse said sternly.

"Well, it is the woods," RJ pointed out. "If this were the city, I wouldn't think so, but there are a lot of animals that live in the woods."

"Listen, Mr. Louis is gone and we need to find him," Mouse said firmly. "I don't care if it was a bear or an alien, but we need to find out what happened."

RJ sighed heavily and shook his head. "Mouse aliens aren't real."

Mouse rolled his eyes and stalked off across the campground.

"I'm going to find him with or without your help!" he called over his shoulder.

"Don't worry Mouse, we'll help!" Rebekah called after him. She looked back at her cousin to see if he was coming too, but saw that he was staring at something in his hand. She noticed the sparkle. It was the glittery guitar pick they had found in the woods the day before!

"Oh no," Rebekah said quietly.

"Oh no is right," RJ agreed as he held the guitar pick up into the air. "I think Bertha might just be involved after all."

"Maybe he just dropped it," Rebekah pointed out.

"Why would he have been all the way out in the woods though?" RJ asked. "It seems a little strange to me."

"Me too," Rebekah agreed. "Come on…let's tell Mouse we're on the case!"

Chapter 5

"Mouse, wait!" Rebekah shouted as she chased after him.

"What are you kids doing running around camp?" a counselor asked as she spotted them. "You should be getting in line for breakfast."

"But, we have to find-" Mouse began to say.

"You don't have to find anything until after breakfast," she said sternly. "There are dangers in the woods, you can't just go running off like this. You guys have been here before, you should know the rules."

"I'm sorry Ms. Cindy," Rebekah said quickly. "We just thought that we saw something in the woods."

"Yes," RJ said as he looked at the counselor. "And I heard some strange noises outside of my cabin last night."

"It was probably just squirrels," Ms. Cindy said. "There are lots of squirrels around here."

"You don't think it could have been a bear?" RJ asked boldly and tilted up the brim of his hat.

"A bear?" Ms. Cindy laughed and shook her head. "I think you three have heard too many scary stories. Go back to your cabins, get dressed and be at breakfast in five minutes or no swimming today!"

She walked off toward the dining hall.

"See, no bears," RJ shrugged as he turned toward his cabin.

"Don't you think that's what any grown up would tell a kid?" Rebekah pointed out. "Remember that boy said they didn't want the little kids to know about it."

"Well," RJ shrugged. "I'm not a little kid."

Rebekah frowned as she ran off to her cabin to change out of her pajamas. Once she was dressed she met Mouse and RJ for breakfast. Mouse was wiggling around in his seat.

"Hurry up and eat, we have to find out what happened to Mr. Louis."

"And how are we going to do that?" RJ asked.

"There has to be a way to prove that he's missing and that he didn't just leave," Rebekah said thoughtfully.

"We have this," RJ said and laid the sparkly guitar pick on the table.

"But we don't even know for sure if it belonged to him," Rebekah pointed out. "The counselors are not going to believe us with just that. We need to find some proof."

"You're absolutely right, little cuz," RJ nodded. "You really are getting good at this detective work."

"Thanks," Rebekah beamed.

Mouse sneaked some of the cheese from his egg sandwich to the mouse in his pocket.

"But how are we going to get proof? What proof might there be?" Mouse asked.

"Well, RJ heard noises outside of your cabin, so maybe it was the bear. If it was the bear, it should have left proof behind," she smirked.

"Oh gross, I'm not looking for bear poop," Mouse said sternly.

"No, ugh," Rebekah groaned. "I meant footprints!"

"Paw prints," RJ corrected smugly.

"So it's agreed?" Rebekah asked hopefully. "As soon as we can, we'll get away from the activities and see if we can find any bear tracks," she glowered at RJ.

It was not easy to get away from the counselors as the first full day of camp was packed with activities. But one hour was set aside for nature time, and the campers were allowed to explore the woods as long as they did so in groups and didn't go past a certain point. As soon as they were allowed to go into the woods, Rebekah, Mouse, and RJ doubled back and headed for the boys' cabin. They walked around behind the cabin searching through the grass and fallen leaves for any sign of a bear.

"I don't see anything," Rebekah frowned.

"I do," RJ sighed as he pointed to a family of squirrels running up and down a nearby tree. "Ms. Cindy was right and that must have been what I heard after all."

"Great," Mouse frowned. "Now how will we find Mr. Louis?"

"Maybe we should go back to where we found the guitar pick," Rebekah said. "If it is his, maybe we can find some tracks there."

"Bear tracks?" Mouse asked nervously.

"Maybe, or maybe Mr. Louis's tracks," she said.

Chapter 6

The three moved through the woods as quickly and quietly as they could. They were past the boundaries the counselors had set and if they were caught, they would be banned from swimming and even campfire activities. When they reached the part of the woods where they had found the guitar pick, RJ held up his hands.

"Now everybody freeze. Until we know what happened to Mr. Louis, this is officially a crime scene. There could be evidence all over the place!"

He whipped out a magnifying glass that had also come in his detective kit and began looking over the leaves on the ground.

"I'll look for claw marks on the trees," Mouse suggested.

Rebekah had her eye on something else. She had noticed a broken twig in the middle of some crushed leaves. She crouched down beside it and looked at it more closely. Not far from it she saw something in the dirt.

"Look!" she cried out happily. "Look what I found!"

The two boys ran over to her to see what she had discovered. It was a shoe print.

"So if it belongs to Mr. Louis, then he wasn't attacked by a bear," Mouse said with relief.

"But just what was he doing out in the woods, alone?" RJ asked suspiciously. "Doesn't seem like a normal thing for a counselor to be doing."

"Well, let's find out!" Rebekah said as she began to follow the footprints. They led a little further into the woods and then down a trail. The trail was very overgrown with bushes. It looked as if no one had walked down it except Mr. Louis in quite some time.

"Where was he going?" Mouse asked with confusion.

"Ouch!" Rebekah frowned as a thorn in one of the bushes scraped her arm. "Doesn't seem like a nice walk in the woods, that's for sure."

The trail ended at the edge of a clearing. There was nothing but dirt and a few shrubs to see. But there were no more footprints!

"How is this possible?" RJ muttered to himself as he inspected the dirt closely with his magnifying glass.

"He couldn't have just stopped walking," Rebekah whispered.

"Unless," Mouse said hesitantly.

"Unless what?" RJ asked as he and Rebekah looked at him.

"Unless he was carried," Mouse said sadly. "By a Bertha."

RJ and Rebekah exchanged worried frowns at Mouse's words. As much as Rebekah didn't want to believe that a bear had carried off Mr. Louis, she also couldn't see another explanation.

"Well somehow he stopped making footprints," Rebekah shook her had.

"But there aren't any bear tracks either," RJ pointed out. "There's no tracks at all, except our own."

"Well that's great," Rebekah suddenly said. "That means we've solved our mystery!"

"What?" RJ said with surprise.

"How do you figure?" Mouse demanded.

“We wanted to find Mr. Louis and we have,” Rebekah said sternly. “A person can't just disappear. So Mr. Louis has to be here somewhere.”

“Maybe he turned into a squirrel,” Mouse suggested with a shrug.

“Really?” RJ asked with an arched brow.

“Mouse,” Rebekah sighed and smacked her forehead. “He's not a squirrel.”

"So you're saying he has to be here somewhere," RJ said softly. "Well maybe he didn't turn into a squirrel, but he might have climbed a tree."

They all took turns looking as high up into the trees around them as they could, but there was no sign of a camp counselor who thought he was a squirrel.

"If he's not in the trees, then where is he?" Rebekah said with frustration. She knew that they had already been gone far too long. Soon the counselors would come looking for them, and all they had for an explanation for breaking the rules was a glittery guitar pick. Mouse sat down on a large fallen tree limb and sighed.

"No one is going to believe us and poor Mr. Louis will never be found."

"What if there isn't anything to believe?" RJ pointed out. "So far all we found for evidence was some foot prints, that may not even belong to Mr. Louis."

"That's true," Rebekah nodded. "But I think Mouse is right. Something tells me Mr. Louis is in trouble and we need to find him."

"Hunches are important," RJ nodded. "But they're not everything Rebekah, you need some real evidence to back them up."

Mouse sighed heavily again. He slumped forward, resting his elbows on his knees. When he did, his mouse escaped the front pocket of his shirt. It went running across the dirt.

"Ah!" RJ shrieked and jumped up into the air as the mouse scuttled by his feet. "Get that thing! Get it, get it!" he demanded as he jumped up and grabbed a low tree limb so that he could get away from the mouse.

"Relax it's just a little mouse," Rebekah couldn't help but giggle.

"I don't like mice!" RJ grumbled as he continued to swing from the tree limb. Mouse had jumped up to chase his little friend.

"Come back here!" he demanded as he ran after the mouse. "I've already lost Mr. Louis, I can't lose you too!"

Chapter 7

As Mouse ran after his pet, they all heard voices calling out through the woods.

"Oh no they're looking for us!" Rebekah winced. "We are going to be in big trouble."

"And we didn't even find Mr. Louis," RJ shook his head.

Rebekah knew if she didn't call out where they were, they would be in even more trouble. So she shouted to the searchers.

"We're here, we're okay!"

As soon as the words were out of her mouth she heard a loud thump. She spun on her heel to see that Mouse had chased his pet into some thick brush at the edge of the trail. But the thump had not come from him running into bushes, that was for sure!

He rubbed his forehead. "Ouch," he muttered.

"What happened?" RJ asked.

"I don't know," Mouse shook his head. "There's something behind the bushes."

"What?" Rebekah asked curiously and started to pull the bushes back. All three of them began tugging at the branches and leaves. Soon they found that the bushes had grown up around an old wooden shack.

"Wow!" Rebekah announced when she felt the wood under her fingertips. "I never would have known this was here."

"Look, that must be where my mouse went," Mouse said as he pointed to a small hole in the bottom of the wooden shack. "We have to get inside! I can't leave without him."

The counselors were getting much closer, and Rebekah knew that they wouldn't be happy that Mouse had brought a pet with him. They would make him go back to his cabin without his friend. She couldn't let that happen to Mouse.

"Alright, let's see if there's a way in," Rebekah said quickly. They pulled harder at the bushes until they found a door.

"This must be it," Rebekah said as she tugged at the wooden handle on the front of the door. But the door wouldn't budge. A large thick branch of the bushes was pinning the door shut.

"Hello?" a voice called out from inside the shack. "Hello is there someone out there?"

Rebekah, Mouse, and RJ all froze at the sound of the voice.

"Do you think that's Magellan?" Mouse whispered.

"No silly," Rebekah laughed. "It must be Mr. Louis! Mr. Louis, is that you?" she called out into the shack.

"Yes it is!" Mr. Louis called out. "Oh please help me get out, I've been stuck in here all night!"

Rebekah, RJ, and Mouse teamed up to tug at the branch. They pulled as hard as they could and were able to get the door part of the way open. Mr. Louis gasped as light spilled into the dark shack that he had been stuck inside of.

"I'm so glad you kids found me," he said. He began pushing back against the door as they pulled, in an attempt to get the door all the way open.

"This isn't working," RJ frowned. "We need to all push together!"

All three wedged themselves inside the door one by one, so that they could push with all their might against the door with Mr. Louis. But while they were pushing hard, the branch of the bush was pushing back just as hard.

"Can you get out Mr. Louis?" Rebekah asked through gritted teeth.

"No, I'm sorry," Mr. Louis sighed. "You are much smaller than me, I can't fit through there!"

RJ lost his footing in the loose dirt, and knocked accidentally into Rebekah who lost her footing too. As they tried to get their balance, they weren't leaning their weight against the door anymore. With only Mouse left to push on the door along with some help from Mr. Louis the door snapped shut once more.

"No, no!" Rebekah cried out as she tried to shove her weight against the door again, but it was too late. When it closed, it trapped all of them inside! In the shadows of the shack, all three kids and Mr. Louis groaned at their situation.

"Now how will we get out?" Mr. Louis sighed.

"We'll find a way," Rebekah said with determination. Mouse was busy looking around the shack.

"What are you looking for?" RJ asked.

"For Magellan!" Mouse replied as he searched the floor of the shack.

"Oh no that mouse is in here with us!" RJ gasped. He began dancing from one foot to the other.

"Mr. Louis what were you doing in here?" Rebekah asked as she shoved on the door, hoping that it would open.

"Well I wanted to put on a really special magic show for you guys, and I had heard rumors about this shack being out here. I thought if I found it, maybe I could use it for a disappearing act," he frowned.

"Well you sure did!" Mouse laughed as he scooped up a squeaking squirming mouse and dropped him into his front pocket. RJ sighed with relief.

Mr. Louis nodded. “I pried the door open, but it slammed shut before I could stop it, and then I couldn't get back out.”

“Now we're all stuck,” Mouse pointed out with a sigh.

“Hey, where did you kids go?” Ms. Cindy shouted from just outside the shack. The counselors were still looking for them!

“Come on everyone,” Rebekah said quickly. “Let's make as much noise as we can!”

They banged on the wooden frame of the shack and shouted at the same time.

“We're in here! We're in here! Under the bushes!”

Chapter 8

The counselors soon discovered the hidden shack. They worked together to pull the branch of the bush that held down the door free. When the door swung open, Rebekah, RJ, and Mouse stepped out, followed by Mr. Louis.

"Louis, what are you doing in there?" Ms. Cindy asked with surprise. "We all thought that you went home early!"

"Luckily for me these kids came looking for me," Mr. Louis said with a shake of his head. "Otherwise I might have been stuck in that shack for a very long time."

"Well Louis," Ms. Cindy said with a frown. "We have rules at this camp you know. We follow the buddy system for a reason!"

Mr. Louis nodded with a sigh. Rebekah was surprised that Mr. Louis was the one getting into trouble. She held her breath as she wondered if they would be next.

"And as for you three," Ms. Cindy said as she crossed her arms and stared at them. "Well you're just regular heroes! Thanks to you Mr. Louis is safe! You should be very proud of yourselves."

Rebekah beamed, as did Mouse. But RJ only shrugged.

"Well I am a junior detective, after all," he said with a slight huff.

"You three have been so brave, I'll make sure I tell the cook to give you each extra desert!" Ms. Cindy announced happily.

"Fantastic!" Mouse said happily.

"Great," Rebekah cringed. She wondered just how much bread pudding Mouse could eat.

That night at dinner, Ms. Cindy announced to all of the campers and other counselors that Rebekah, Mouse, and RJ had rescued Mr. Louis.

"We should all give them a round of applause!"

All of the other campers cheered and clapped for them. Rebekah felt very proud. Mouse barely noticed as he was too busy with three dishes of bread pudding in front of them. RJ smiled at Rebekah and gave her a thumbs up.

"Good work little cuz," he said. "We make a great team!"

At the end of the week, Mouse and Mr. Louis had another treat for the campers. They put on the greatest magic show ever.

"Now, I will make this little mouse disappear," Mr. Louis announced and waved his magic wand over Magellan.

"I don't care where it goes, as long as it stays away from me!" RJ cringed. Rebekah laughed and waited with everyone else to see just where Magellan would show up.

"Oh dear," Mr. Louis said as he lifted the box and discovered that there was no mouse underneath. "It seems our little mouse might be missing," he sighed dramatically. Rebekah suspected it was all part of the act. RJ pulled his feet up on to the bleachers. Then his eyes widened.

"Rebekah," he squeaked. "Is my hat moving?"

Rebekah looked up at his brown detective hat and gasped. It was indeed wiggling back and forth on his head.

"Ah!" RJ cried out and snatched his hat off of the top of his head.

"There he is!" all the kids cheered.

"Don't worry RJ, I'll save you!" Rebekah declared. She scooped Magellan up out of his thick red hair. "See, no more little mouse," she grinned.

"My hero!" RJ sighed as he sat back down.

Rebekah couldn't have been prouder.

Rebekah - Girl Detective #10
Zombie Burgers
PJ Ryan

Rebekah - Girl Detective #10

Zombie Burgers

Chapter 1

The pen could not have moved any faster across her notebook. She kept scribbling away. Rebekah was sitting at her usual lunch table. She had it reserved since the first grade. She was watching the new cook in the cafeteria who was limping as she walked between the tables. It was Rebekah's third day as a fourth grader, and already she felt much smarter. Especially since she was the only one to discover that the new lunch lady was a zombie. There was no question about it. Rebekah scribbled another note as the cook walked the line of food. She moved very slowly. Whenever she walked she stumbled a little. At one point she almost lost her balance and let out a long low groan.

Rebekah added to her notebook: Walks like a zombie, Groans like a zombie.

She tapped her pen lightly as the other students around her happily ate their meals. Rebekah hadn't touched her food. Her stomach was churning over the idea of the lunch lady being a zombie. The only thing she couldn't figure out was why would a zombie want to work in a school cafeteria? What could she be after? Maybe she was hiding out, and trying to blend in. Or maybe she was out for something tasty, that wasn't on the lunch menu, like brains! What better brains could there be than brains of kids in school? They were active and growing kids walking from classroom to classroom. She imagined they would have to be pretty tasty to zombies.

Brains? Rebekah scribbled down in her notebook.

"Brains?" Mouse asked as he sat down beside her with a frown. "What is that supposed to mean?"

Rebekah glanced up at her best friend, and narrowed her eyes. Out of the top pocket of Mouse's shirt a little white mouse stuck out its tiny pink nose.

"Nothing," she said and wrapped her arm around her notebook. She didn't want him to see.

"What is it?" he asked more firmly. "Let me see!" he tugged at her arm and tried to catch a glimpse of what she had written.

"Fine," Rebekah said and pushed the notebook toward him with a huff. As Mouse read over her notes, his eyes got wider and wider. Rebekah continued to tap the pen, this time on the table. She watched as the woman walked back toward the kitchen. Mouse looked up at the woman she was watching and shook his head.

Chapter 2

"Her name is Mrs. Rosado, and she is not a zombie," Mouse said confidently.

"How do you know?" Rebekah asked.

"Because I met her on the first day. I always ask for any leftover cheese for my mice, and she was very nice. She said she would save it for me," he smiled. "What kind of zombie would save me cheese?"

"You didn't see, what I saw," Rebekah pointed out.

"No, no! School just started Rebekah, our books won't even open all the way yet, you can't be accusing the lunch lady of being a zombie!" he smacked his forehead and groaned.

Rebekah cleared her throat. "On the first day of school I saw her walking funny down the hall."

"Most grown ups walk funny," Mouse pointed out. "They're always wearing weird shoes."

"Well I, being the courteous person I am, followed her to offer some help, since was having a hard time," Rebekah explained.

'Of course," Mouse nodded slightly.

"Well she went to a side door near the kitchen. She opened it. There was this man that I've never seen before," Rebekah said.

"Okay, well there are a lot of men in the world," Mouse shrugged.

"This man was very pale," Rebekah explained in a lowered voice.

"Lots of people are pale Rebekah," Mouse sighed.

"He also wore very old clothes," Rebekah said.

"Lots of people wear old clothes too," Mouse interrupted, getting frustrated.

“Oh really, well do lots of men walk off across the field of the school with their arms held out like this?” Rebekah stretched her arms straight out in front of her. When she glanced up she saw Mrs. Rosado staring at her. She dropped her arms quickly back to her sides.

“Seriously?” Mouse asked. He had no explanation for why someone would be walking across a field like that.

“So, she's a zombie,” Rebekah said with a nod. “Probably the queen zombie!”

Mouse shook his head fast from side to side. “No! She's not a zombie!”

Rebekah met Mouse's eyes and smirked. “Prove it.”

Mouse sighed and nodded. “Alright, I'll show you. We'll spy on her. You'll see she's not doing anything in the kitchen but making food.”

“Eat your food children!” a voice said from right behind them. Rebekah nearly jumped out of her chair when she looked over her shoulder and saw that it was Mrs. Rosado. She opened her mouth to speak, but all that came out was a little squeak.

“Yes ma'am,” Mouse said with a charming smile. Mrs. Rosado moved on to the next table. Once all of the students were done eating their food Mouse and Rebekah hung out near the kitchen door. Mrs. Rosado was busy preparing lunch for the next day. She was dumping lots of hamburger meat into a big bowl.

“Yum, burgers are my favorite!” Mouse whispered to Rebekah. Just then they both heard a grinding sound. It was very loud. Mrs. Rosado stepped back into view carrying the pitcher from the blender. It was filled with a green frothy substance, almost like a goo.

“Uh, what is that?” Rebekah asked and scrunched up her nose.

"She's not going to-" Mouse started to say as Mrs. Rosado walked up to the bowl of hamburger meat. Before he could finish his sentence Mrs. Rosado dumped all of the green goo into the hamburger meat. Mouse was horrified and nearly slumped over in shock. Rebekah held his arm to keep him standing. Mrs. Rosado laughed as she stirred the hamburger meat.

"They'll never even know," she smirked. She glanced in the direction of the kitchen door. Rebekah and Mouse ducked out of the way swiftly. They were out of sight just in time.

"Let's get out of here," Mouse groaned. "I think my tummy is upset."

"Mine too," Rebekah narrowed her eyes. "What are the chances of having a zombie for a cook?"

"Now wait," Mouse said with a frown. "We still don't know for sure that she's a zombie. We need to look back at our evidence."

"You're right," Rebekah agreed and pulled her notebook out of her pocket. Together they looked over the list of evidence that they already had.

"She talks to zombies," Rebekah said.

"Or a man that look like a zombie," Mouse pointed out.

"She walks like a zombie," Rebekah said.

"Or she wears funny shoes," Mouse reminded her.

"And now, she put zombie goo in the hamburger meat!" Rebekah declared.

Mouse opened his mouth, but then he shook his head. "That one I can't argue with."

"So what are we going to do about it?" Rebekah asked with a scowl.

"What can we do?" Mouse sighed and glanced over his shoulder in the direction of the cafeteria. "It's not like anyone is going to believe us. Just in case she is a zombie, we probably shouldn't make her mad by accusing her. So what can we do?"

Rebekah narrowed her eyes thoughtfully. "Well we have to do something!" she announced.

Chapter 3

That afternoon when she got home from school, her mind was filled with ideas of how to stop the zombie. Maybe she could make a zombie trap. Maybe she could find a zombie hunter that specialized in such things.

One thing she knew for sure was that she couldn't sit by while Mrs. Rosado pretended not to be a zombie. In fact, she had to wonder why a zombie would want to work in a school lunch room. What was she planning?

Rebekah could barely eat her dinner. She kept thinking of that green goo. Would it hurt the students? Had she sneaked it into other meals at school? When she went to bed that night, Rebekah was still trying to figure it out. Of course Mrs. Rosado was a zombie, but why would a zombie be a lunch lady? It just didn't make sense.

Rebekah fell asleep thinking of this. Sometime during the night she heard a tapping. At first it was a tapping, and then it sounded more like a scratching. She woke with a start and looked at her window. The curtains were drawn. There was a long shadow behind them. It looked like an arm that was reaching for her window. Rebekah was scared, but she had to see what it was. She held her breath as she crept over to the window. She grabbed the edges of the curtains and closed her eyes tightly.

"Please don't be a zombie, please don't be a zombie," she said under her breath. All at once she pulled the curtains back. The tapping and scratching wasn't from a zombie at all. It was a branch from the tree beside her window. But there was a zombie! At least, what looked like zombie! A zombie with wild red hair and wide scared eyes.

"Oh no!" Rebekah gasped. "It's me!" It was her reflection in the window that she had thought was a zombie.

Tired from not sleeping all night, Rebekah's face was very pale. She crawled back into bed, her mind still spinning with fear. That's when she realized what Mrs. Rosado was up to. She wasn't there to cook food for children. She was there to turn the children into an army of zombies!

Chapter 4

When Rebekah arrived at school the next day she was more determined than ever to put a stop to the zombie lunch lady. She had the entire school to protect! Mouse caught up with her in the hallway just before class.

"Hi Rebekah," he said cheerfully. His smile faded when he saw her scowl. Even the mouse in his pocket ducked down to avoid it. "I guess we're still thinking the lunch lady is a zombie," he sighed.

"Not only is she a zombie," Rebekah said as she slammed her locker shut and began marching down the hall. "She's trying to turn all of us into zombies too! That's what that goo was!"

Mouse frowned as they entered their first class of the day. "Well it is strange that she would try to hide it from everyone."

"Settle down class," the teacher announced from the front of the room. "Please listen to the morning announcements."

The PA system squawked to life and a tinny voice carried through the speakers.

"Today's lunch will be a special treat, hamburgers and french fries!" the voice announced. Rebekah and Mouse looked at each other with wide eyes. The tinny voice went on to list the clubs that would be meeting after school.

"I told you!" Rebekah hissed at Mouse. "What kind of school lunch doesn't even have vegetables?" she pointed out. "It's all a big trick to make us eat the hamburgers."

Mouse nodded slowly. "I think you might be right about this one Rebekah. But aren't we in over our heads? Maybe we should call your cousin RJ?"

Rebekah shook her head as she folded her arms. "No way. We can handle this ourselves."

"But how?" Mouse asked.

"All I know for sure is that no one is going to eat those hamburgers today!" Rebekah said sternly.

Mouse nodded as if he agreed, but he looked a little worried too. Rebekah always had a way of getting them both into trouble with her detective work.

Chapter 5

At lunch time, Rebekah marched into the cafeteria. She was determined to stop the students from eating the hamburgers. She knew that one bite might be the last real meal they ever had. Once they were zombies who knew what they would eat. As she looked around at all the children milling about, excited about having hamburgers and french fries for lunch, she felt bad for them. They were going to miss out on a delicious treat. But it was for their own good. Rebekah walked boldly up to the lunch line. Mrs. Rosado was standing behind the counter ready to serve her zombie hamburgers.

"I know what you did," Rebekah hissed at her. Mrs. Rosado raised an eyebrow.

"Excuse me?" she said. "What did I do?"

"I'm not going to let it happen. I'm going to stop you. So you might as well whip out the peanut butter and jelly sandwiches right now!"

Mrs. Rosado gritted her teeth and took a deep breath as if she was trying very hard to be patient.

"Would you please move along and collect your food. Other students are waiting," she pointed to the line forming behind Rebekah.

"Do not eat these hamburgers!" Rebekah announced to the line of students. But they weren't listening. They smelled the french fries and the toasted buns. They pushed past Rebekah ready to feast.

"Oh no!" Rebekah gasped. She had really thought that the other kids would listen to her. She expected they would line up behind her and march right out of the cafeteria in protest. But apparently eating french fries was more important than not becoming a zombie! Rebekah tried to grab the attention of the kids leaving the lunch line with their tray.

"Don't eat it!" Rebekah pleaded. "She put zombie goo in it! It will turn you into a zombie!"

Most of the kids seemed to think that Rebekah was joking. Or maybe that she had somehow gone insane. They all just laughed at her and carried their trays to their tables. Mouse entered the cafeteria just as Rebekah was going into a full panic. He saw the wildness in her eyes and braced himself for what might happen next. Soon the lunch room tables were filling with trays and students ready to eat. Things were getting out of control and fast. Rebekah could only think of one thing to do. She went to the fullest table and stood in front of it.

"This is for your own good!" she promised the students who stared at her with confusion. Rebekah jumped up on top of the table, knocking off trays and cartons of milk as she did.

"No one eat the burgers!" she shouted again and again. "No one eat the burgers, they're no good! They are filled with goo!"

Mrs. Rosado came running out from behind the counter to see what was happening.

"Oh no!" she shrieked when she saw the mess that Rebekah was making. "What have you done?" she demanded.

“I told you I would stop you,” Rebekah said with a smirk as she jumped from table to table. She kicked off all the trays with hamburgers. The kids were staring at her in horror as they all tried to guess just how much trouble she would be in. Mouse hung his head and tried to disappear. He hoped that Rebekah wouldn't expect him to jump on the tables now. Mrs. Rosado chased after Rebekah the best she could with her limp.

"Stop that," she shouted as Rebekah kicked off another tray. "Stop that right now!”

Rebekah jumped on to another table before the lunch lady could catch her. She sent all the trays scattering from one end of the table. Someone must have gone to fetch the principal Mr. Powers, because it was his voice that boomed across the cafeteria.

“Stop this nonsense right now!” he shouted. Rebekah ducked and turned to face him. She was obviously the guilty party, since she was standing on top of a lunch room table.

“Get down this instant,” Mr. Powers snapped as he folded his arms across his chest. Mrs. Rosado smirked as Rebekah reluctantly climbed down off of the table.

“Young lady, it is the fourth day of school, isn't it?” Mr. Powers asked with a raised eyebrow.

“Yes sir,” she said solemnly.

“We couldn't get through one week without a food fight?” he asked sharply.

“It's just the hamburgers-” Rebekah started to say.

“In my office, now,” he said sternly and then looked at the other students. “I'm sure that Mrs. Rosado can provide each of you with a nice peanut butter and jelly sandwich. You may eat out on the playground, just for today, since the cafeteria will need to be cleaned.”

Rebekah received quite a few glares from the other students. They had all been looking forward to their hamburgers and french fries.

"Let's go," he said to Rebekah and marched out of the cafeteria. Mouse waved slightly to Rebekah who sent him a frown that made it seem as if she was doomed.

Chapter 6

Mr. Powers' office was very neat and tidy. Everything had its place. Even Rebekah who sat down right in front of his desk.

"Now Rebekah," Mr. Powers said sternly. "I understand if you feel strongly about being a vegetarian."

Rebekah's eyes widened, but she did not correct him, she only nodded her head.

"Yes Mr. Powers," she said with a frown.

"I'm not a big fan of meat myself," Mr. Powers said with a shrug. "But you can't expect everyone else at the school to follow your same diet. Okay?"

“Yes sir,” Rebekah said shifting in her chair. “So I'm not in trouble?”

“Well I can't have you making a scene like you did today again, young lady,” the principal warned. “But I think if you go and help Mrs. Rosado clean up the mess you made that I can let you slide this time.”

Rebekah shuddered at the idea of having to be alone with the zombie lunch lady, but she nodded. “Yes sir,” she said. At least she wouldn't be getting a detention.

As she stood up from her chair and walked toward the door of the office, she spotted a man walking down the hallway. He was very pale, and wore old and dirty clothes. She knew she was supposed to go back to the cafeteria, but she couldn't let a zombie wander the school!

She followed after the man through the empty hallways. When she saw him pause beside a utility closet she ducked behind a bank of lockers. The man glanced around once and then unlocked the door. He stepped inside of the closet.

Rebekah ran up to the closet and peeked inside the small window. She wanted to know what he was doing in there. Was he storing the zombie goo for Mrs. Rosado? Was he hatching some other terrible plan? To her surprise, there was no one in there!

How could he have just disappeared? Was he a zombie ghost? A zombie magician? She had no idea what to think. But she was sure that if she didn't get back to the cafeteria and help Mrs. Rosado she would end up in detention after all. She ran down the hall back toward the cafeteria, her mind brimming with explanations for the zombie's disappearance.

When she walked back into the cafeteria it was empty, except for Mrs. Rosado who was leaning over picking up some of the trays that Rebekah had knocked over. As she stood up she let out a loud groan that made Rebekah want to run right back out of the cafeteria. But she knew that the principal would never believe her.

"You," Mrs. Rosado said with a glare. "You clean up this mess!" she said sternly and then stalked back into the kitchen. As Rebekah was cleaning up the trays and the food from the floor she thought about the hamburger meat. She knew that Mrs. Rosado had made a lot more. She was sure that the next day she would be serving hamburgers again. She couldn't let her turn the entire school into zombies. As Rebekah put the last tray back on to the counter, she called out into the kitchen.

"I'm all done!"

Mrs. Rosado came out to inspect her work. As she was checking under the tables for any stray french fries, Rebekah ducked into the kitchen. She found the bowl of hamburger meat and tossed it out in the garbage. Then she slipped back out.

"Fine," Mrs. Rosado said with a huff. "Don't do that again!" she insisted. "You may not like my cooking, but it is very rude to make such a scene. It is even worse to try to cause all of the other kids to feel the same way."

Rebekah nodded, her heart pounding. "I'm sorry," she said through gritted teeth. She hoped Mrs. Rosado wouldn't notice the hamburger meat was thrown out while she was still there. "Go to class," Mrs. Rosado instructed. She placed her hands on her hips and watched as Rebekah left the cafeteria. Rebekah could feel her zombie eyes on her back the entire way.

Chapter 7

Rebekah ran all the way to her next class. It had already started, and the teacher waved her inside. He tried to hide a smirk of amusement. He had heard about her antics in the cafeteria. Mouse was waiting there for her, her desk saved so that she could sit next to him. She slumped down at the desk, her features creased by a frown.

"I can't believe how brave you were," he whispered to her once she was settled.

"I don't know about brave," Rebekah shivered as she recalled the feeling of zombie eyes watching her. "But luckily I didn't get detention."

"How did you manage that?" Mouse asked with surprise. He was certain she would have a year's worth of detention.

"Mr. Powers thinks I'm a vegetation," Rebekah giggled behind her hand. Mouse rolled his eyes and shook his head.

"Good one Rebekah," he mumbled.

When class was over it was almost time to go home. They began walking down the hallway toward their lockers to gather what they needed to take home.

"I was thinking," Mouse said with a frown. "If she really is making some kind of zombifying concoction, maybe we can get a sample of it to check it out in the science lab."

"Then we would have evidence!" Rebekah said cheerfully. "Mouse you really are brilliant!" she hugged him tightly.

"I know," Mouse laughed. "Now let go, or you'll squish Boyardee!"

"You named your mouse, Boyardee?" Rebekah asked with surprise.

"Well I found him behind some cans of spaghetti-os," Mouse started to explain and then shook his head. "No time for that, we need to find a way to prove what Mrs. Rosado is up to."

"So how are we going to get a sample?" Rebekah wondered.

"Well if we wait until after the last bell rings for the day we can sneak into the kitchen," Mouse suggested.

"I like the way you think," Rebekah grinned. They hurried off to their last class of the day.

Chapter 8

After the last bell rung they met up in the hall outside of the cafeteria. "Are you ready for this?" Rebekah asked him.

"As ready as I'll ever be," Mouse replied with a nervous smile. "Hopefully she's already gone home for the day."

They leaned around the corner of the kitchen door. The kitchen was empty. They slipped inside and began searching through the kitchen for any of the green goo.

"Ugh look," Mouse said as he pointed to the blender that had a little bit left in the bottom.

"There's our sample," Rebekah cringed at the smell. Just then the kitchen door creaked as if it was about to open. Mouse and Rebekah looked around searching for anywhere to hide. The only option was under the curtained sink. They squished together in the small space and held their breath as the door swung all the way open, with a loud groan. Mouse closed his eyes and Rebekah pushed her head back as she tried to hide. It had to be Mrs. Rosado. They heard her footsteps dragging along the floor as she walked over to the sink. The water turned on for a moment. Then off. Then they heard chopping.

"Get back here you," they heard her hiss. "They won't even know what they're eating, but these kids need a good dose of Mrs. Rosado's special recipe," she giggled shrilly. Then she grew silent for a moment, before adding along with a sharp chop. "Well you're a slimy one, aren't you."

Chop! Chop!

Rebekah cringed and wondered just what she might be slicing up. What went into zombie goo? She wasn't sure, and she did not want to find out. Mrs. Rosado limped away from the sink. They hoped that she had left, but a moment later they heard the grinding of the blender.

“She's making more!” Rebekah hissed. “Our lunches will never be safe!”

Mouse nodded quickly, his face growing pale at the very thought of that green goo being inside of his hamburger. When the grinding stopped, they both waited. Rebekah wished the woman would just leave. Didn't she have other zombie duties to attend to?

"I think she might be gone," Mouse whispered beside Rebekah's ear.

"Are you sure?" Rebekah whispered back, feeling very worried that they might walk into a trap.

"Only one way to find out," Mouse replied quietly. He began to pull aside the curtain on the sink. Rebekah winced, hoping that they would not be caught. Before Mouse could even get the curtain all the way open, Boyardee slid out of his shirt pocket. It was easy for the mouse to do because Mouse was leaning over, looking for the lunch lady's shoes.

Chapter 9

"No Boyardee!" Mouse hissed. "Come back here you bad mouse!"

But the little white mouse was just a blur as he bolted across the kitchen floor. Suddenly they heard a shriek.

"A mouse in my kitchen?" Mrs. Rosado fumed. "Never!" they heard her limping quickly after the mouse.

"No, no," Mouse sobbed. "She's going to turn Boyardee into a zombie mouse!"

Rebekah frowned. She knew how much Mouse's mice meant to him. She also knew that a zombie mouse would not be nearly as fun. Bravely she stepped out from under the sink to rescue the mouse. All of Mrs. Rosado's shrieking and hollering had reached the ears of her zombie friend. When Rebekah stepped out from under the sink they were both chasing the mouse.

"Leave that mouse alone!" Rebekah declared loudly.

"You again!" Mrs. Rosado threw her hands up into the air. "Why are you doing this to me?"

"Why am I doing this to you?" Rebekah asked with surprise. 'Why are you doing this to us? Why did you have to pick our school for your army of zombies?"

Mrs. Rosado stared at her as if she had sprouted a carrot out of the top of her head. She shook her head slowly.

"Say that again?" she asked.

"I said, why did you have to pick our school to create your army of zombies?" Rebekah repeated and then shot a glare in the other zombie's direction.

"Why would you ever think I was making an army of zombies?" Mrs. Rosado asked, so dumbfounded that she couldn't even be angry.

"Well, let's just see why," Rebekah said sharply. She whipped out her detective notebook and began to read off the list of evidence. Meanwhile Mouse started hunting for Boyardee.

"You walk like a zombie," Rebekah explained. "You groan like a zombie, you talk to zombies," she pointed at the man standing beside Mrs. Rosado. "You created a zombie goo to sneak into our food-"

"Zombie goo?" Mrs. Rosado said with a short laugh. Then her eyes lit up. "Do you mean this?" she asked as she picked up the blender pitcher filled with frothy green goo.

"Yes that," Rebekah said and then covered her mouth with both hands. She made noises behind her hand that sounded like, 'I won't drink it'.

"This is not zombie goo," Mrs. Rosado said with another laugh. "This is vegetables," she pointed to the broccoli, peppers, celery, and cucumbers that she had used to create the concoction. "I just thought it would be a good way to make sure that all of you kids were getting a good helping of vegetables each day," she explained with a trembling smile. "I can't believe that you thought I was a zombie!"

"What about your limp and your groan?" Rebekah asked, still not convinced. Mouse walked up beside her with Boyardee captured in his hands.

"Yes, and this zombie," Mouse pointed at the man beside Mrs. Rosado. "Rebekah saw him walking with his arms straight out in front of him."

"Mr. Baker is not a zombie either," Mrs. Rosado said sternly. "Now listen, I think it's great for kids to have imaginations, but you two take the cake with this one. I have a limp because my back is bad, and I groan and moan because sometimes when I lift things or bend over, it hurts."

"And I am the new groundskeeper and janitor for the school," Mr. Baker said with a shake of his head. "When you saw me, I was doing a special exercise for my arms. I spent a lot of time in the basement this past week stacking and emptying boxes so my arms were sore. Mrs. Rosado taught me an exercise that her doctor taught her, to help with her back."

Rebekah sighed as all of the pieces of the puzzle began to come together. Mr. Baker was pale because he worked in the basement so often. "And I guess the entrance to the basement is in the utility closet?" Rebekah asked with a grimace.

"Yes it is," he nodded slightly. "How did you know that?"

"I might have followed you," Rebekah said quietly. "I might have thought you were a zombie ghost because you disappeared in the closet."

"A zombie ghost," Mr. Baker laughed at that. "Well you are a creative one."

"So just to be clear," Mrs. Rosado said with a point of her finger. "I am not a zombie and neither is Mr. Baker."

"Yes ma'am," Rebekah said quietly.

"Yes ma'am," Mouse agreed. "But I still don't want vegetable goo in my hamburgers!"

"Are you going to tell Mr. Powers?" Rebekah asked nervously. She knew that he wouldn't be so nice with a second offense.

"Hm," Mrs. Rosado said. "I'll make you a deal. If you two promise not to tell the other kids what I sneak in their hamburgers, then I promise not to tell Mr. Powers about this little incident."

Rebekah nodded solemnly. "It's a deal," she said.

As Rebekah and Mouse started to walk out of the kitchen, Mrs. Rosado called after them.

"And keep that mouse out of my kitchen!"

Rebekah - Girl Detective #11
Mouse's Secret
MICE ONLY
PJ Ryan

Rebekah - Girl Detective #11

Mouse's Secret

Chapter 1

Rebekah was sprawled out across her bed, flipping through a new book that her cousin RJ had sent her in the mail. It was a book all about famous detectives throughout history. Rebekah thought of herself as a girl detective. Her cousin RJ was a detective too and he was always on the look-out for tips and advice to share with Rebekah. So far the book was interesting, but it was very thick. It had a lot of pages and Rebekah couldn't understand some of the words. She jotted down the ones she didn't know on a pad of paper so that she could look them up later.

As she read through the stories, she imagined being back in time with these detectives. She could be their trusty assistant. It would have been very interesting to solve mysteries before there were cameras, computers, and telephones. As she flipped to the next page she heard a strange sound. It was a scampering sound. It made her a little nervous. It reminded her of monster claws or the little feet of gremlins.

She sat up on her bed and pulled her feet up on to the bed with her. Bravely, she looked in the direction of the scampering sound. A white blur bolted across the floor of her bedroom. Rebekah's eyes widened and she gasped.

"Mouse!" she called out, but she wasn't yelling at the small white rodent that was now hiding under her bed. She was calling out to her friend Mouse, who she suspected was hiding in the hallway.

"Hi Rebekah!" he grinned as he stepped into her room. Mouse always had a pet mouse with him. He had over twenty mice of his own. He liked to collect them and give them different names. That was how he got his nickname, Mouse. Rebekah had called him that since the first day they met and a mouse had run across her shoe.

"Get him!" Rebekah said as she jumped down from the bed and began searching underneath it for the mouse. "If Mom sees him she will have a fit," she giggled at the thought.

"Don't worry," Mouse smiled as he crouched down and held out a small piece of cheddar cheese. The mouse scampered right out from under the bed and into the palm of Mouse's hand.

"Wow, he's hungry," Rebekah laughed as the mouse scarfed down the entire piece of cheese in a matter of seconds.

"What are you up to today?" Mouse asked. It was Sunday so they had the whole day to play.

"I was just reading," Rebekah shrugged as she held up the book about detectives.

"Nice," he said with a smile. "Did RJ send you that?"

"Yup, but I am ready to take a break," Rebekah grinned. "What are you up to today?"

"I was hoping we could go to the park, I brought my soccer ball," he pointed out into the hallway where a green and black soccer ball was waiting for them.

"Great!" Rebekah grabbed her shoes and put her book carefully on her desk. "And don't forget we have our bowling night on Wednesday," she said quickly as she caught sight of her bowling bag in the corner of her room. She and Mouse had a Wednesday night tradition of going bowling together.

"I won't forget!" Mouse promised. Then she and Mouse ran down the stairs and out of the house.

Chapter 2

Rebekah and Mouse walked down to the park that was not far from where they lived. It had a big grassy field as well as a playground. On the grassy field people would play ball, fly kites, and sometimes do cartwheels and gymnastics. It was a fun place to be, especially on a sunny day.

As Rebekah and Mouse began kicking the ball back and forth, some other kids came over to play too. They all had a game of kick-away which was a lot of fun. In kick-away everyone has to try to kick the ball away from the person who has it. Then whoever kicks it away and gets to it first is the one that everyone else has to kick the ball away from.

There was no way to win really. It was just a way to have fun and it always made everyone laugh and shriek as they tried to kick the ball away. When the other kids had to leave and it was just Mouse and Rebekah again they began tossing the soccer ball back and forth.

"I'm really glad that we came to the park," Rebekah said with a smile.

"Even though there are no mysteries to solve?" Mouse asked with a lop-sided grin.

"Oh there are mysteries," Rebekah said firmly with a glimmer in her green eyes. "There are always mysteries. But it's my day off!"

They both laughed. When Mouse threw the ball toward Rebekah, he caught his foot in a thick patch of grass. He started to fall, so the ball went high over Rebekah's head. Mouse caught himself with his hand, but his pet mouse slipped out of the top pocket of his shirt. The mouse scampered along the grass toward the woods. The ball was rolling in the other direction. Mouse chased after his pet, while Rebekah chased after the ball.

"I'll get it!" she called out and tried to run faster. When she snatched up the ball, she turned around in time to see Mouse chasing his pet right into the woods.

"Do you need help?" she offered.

"I'll get him!" Mouse called over his shoulder as he disappeared into the woods.

Chapter 3

Mouse could easily see his pet as he chased after it. Its white coloring made it stand out against the green and brown leaves that were scattered across the ground in the woods. But catching it was not as easy. The mouse was fast, that's why Mouse had named it Speedy.

"Come back Speedy!" he called out and reached into his pocket for some extra cheese. Mouse and Rebekah had rules to follow while they were at the park. One of those rules was not to go into the woods alone. But Mouse hadn't planned on going so far into the woods. He thought he would catch his pet right away.

He realized as he chased down his mouse that he was getting deeper into the woods than he had ever been before. Finally he caught up with his pet who was burrowing in a pile of leaves. He scooped Speedy up into his hands and dropped him into the front pocket of his shirt. As he did a pine cone knocked him right on the top of the head.

"Ouch!" Mouse growled and glared up at the tree. Of course, the tree hadn't meant to throw a pine cone at him, at least he didn't think so. There was something strange about the tree however. In its branches it looked like something large had been built. It was molded all around the tree. It looked a bit like a small house or a very large tree house.

"It's a tree house!" he gasped and stared up at it with admiration. He had always wanted to build one, but his yard had bushes and not so many trees. It looked like the tree house hadn't been used in some time, but there was still a rope ladder dangling from a branch that would let him climb up and go inside.

"Mouse?" he could hear Rebekah calling for him. He knew if he didn't go back soon she would be worried enough to come looking for him. Then she might get lost in the woods! He wanted to climb up to take a look at the tree house, but he didn't have time at the moment. So as he walked back to the edge of the woods he tried his best to remember exactly how he had gotten to the tree house. Once he stepped outside of the woods, Rebekah was there waiting for him.

"Are you okay?" she asked. "I was about to come look for you."

"I'm fine," Mouse said quickly. "Speedy is fast!"

"Good name then," Rebekah laughed.

Mouse was just about to tell Rebekah about the tree house, when suddenly he didn't want to. He wanted to be the first to explore it. Rebekah was such a good detective, and she always found everything first. He wanted to have the tree house to himself, just for a little while.

To take his mind off of it, he decided to practice one of his new magic tricks.

"Hey did I show you that new magic trick I learned?" he asked with a wide smile. Mouse was very good at magic tricks. Well, he tried to be very good at magic tricks. He wanted to be a magician. He liked the idea of tricking people into believing that something amazing had happened. He was always learning new tricks from books or websites on the computer.

"No you haven't," Rebekah said reluctantly. Rebekah didn't really like magic tricks. She liked mysteries that were meant to be solved, not mysteries that were meant to fool you.

"Oh great, well let me show you!" Mouse said eagerly. He always liked to show off his magic.

"If you must," Rebekah frowned and stood impatiently in front of him.

"Oh," Mouse frowned. "You don't want to see it?"

"Well, I was having fun playing soccer," Rebekah explained as she held up the ball in her hands. "I was hoping we were going to keep playing."

"It won't take long," Mouse promised her. "I think you're really going to like it."

"Mouse," Rebekah shook her head slightly. "You know I don't really like magic tricks."

"Trust me, you'll like this one," Mouse insisted. He began pulling out a long ribbon of cloth from his pocket. Rebekah groaned as that was one of the oldest magic tricks in the books. "What? Did I already show you?" Mouse asked with a confused frown.

"No, but I've seen it before," Rebekah shrugged. She wasn't impressed. Rebekah was always very up front about how she felt, and Mouse knew that she didn't mean to hurt his feelings, but she did. He was upset that she wouldn't just watch one trick.

"Fine," he said sharply. "Forget about it," he shoved the ribbon back into his pocket.

"Great, let's go play!" Rebekah said quickly. She had no idea that she had actually hurt Mouse's feelings.

"No, forget about that too," Mouse said sternly. He took the soccer ball from her. "I'm going home."

"Oh," Rebekah was surprised. "I thought you wanted to play some more?"

"No, I'm going home," Mouse repeated and then stalked off out of the park with his soccer ball tucked under his arm. Rebekah stared after him. She wasn't sure what to think. But she didn't even consider that she might have hurt Mouse's feelings.

Chapter 4

The next morning at school Rebekah waited for Mouse by his locker. They usually met up before classes. But she didn't see him. When the bell rang she had to go to class. She caught glimpses of him during breaks between classes, but he was always walking in the other direction.

The next day at school Mouse didn't meet her at his locker. He also didn't meet her for lunch. She was getting very upset, thinking that he was trying to avoid her. She had never had a hard time finding Mouse before.

At the last bell she stalked right out of school to look for him. She found him around the side of the school near the bicycle racks. He was talking very quietly with a few other kids. Rebekah knew them from school.

There was Amanda, who Rebekah knew from art class. There was also Max who she knew from gym class, and Jaden who she had seen in the lunch room. They were all gathered around Mouse who seemed to be whispering.

As Rebekah got closer, Mouse stopped talking. He looked at her and then turned his head. Rebekah gasped. Mouse had never snubbed her before. What was he talking to the other kids about?

Rebekah was just about to walk over there to find out exactly what was happening, but before she could get over there, Mouse and his friends began marching away. Rebekah was going to call out to him but she knew that he had seen her. She knew that he had decided that he didn't want to talk to her.

Her feelings were very hurt, but more than that, she knew that this was a mystery. She had to find out why Mouse was avoiding her. She had to find out what they had been talking about.

Chapter 5

When Rebekah got home from school, she decided to pay Mouse a visit. She was going to get the truth out of him, even if he was angry with her. So she marched her way to his house. She marched up his sidewalk. She marched up to his front door. Then she knocked on the door.

She was practicing in her head exactly what she would say to him. She would remind him of what good friends they were. She would remind him that she didn't like to be left out. Most of all she would remind him about their bowling night, which was coming up fast. But it wasn't Mouse that opened the door. It was Mouse's mother.

"Oh hi Rebekah," she said with a smile. "Are you looking for Mouse?" she asked.

"Yes I am," Rebekah said firmly, but she had to smile politely at Mouse's mother.

"Well he's already gone to the park," his mother said. "I'm sure he will meet you there."

Rebekah had her feelings hurt all over again. Mouse had gone to the park, their park, without her? Why wouldn't he have invited her to go?

"Thanks," she said sadly, and turned away from the door. She walked toward the park with her shoulders slumped. She couldn't think of a single reason why Mouse would leave her out.

As she got closer to the park, she noticed a group of kids walking in front of her. It was the same kids that she had seen earlier in the day and Mouse was leading the way. Not only had he left her out of going to the park, he had invited all of his new friends instead!

She hung back far enough that they couldn't see her. Then she crept along the bushes and the trees that lined the sidewalk. She followed them until they entered the park. She watched as they skipped the playground. They walked across the grassy field without stopping to play tag. They walked right to the edge of the woods.

Rebekah gasped as she saw Mouse lead the other kids into the woods. The rule was that they were not supposed to go too far into the woods, but Mouse just kept walking. Rebekah knew that she would be seen if she walked right behind them. So she entered the woods from closer to the playground. She had to listen very closely to the sounds of their voices and footsteps. With the crunching of the leaves she could tell which direction they were walking in. When she got closer she spotted something strange. There were pieces of cardboard taped up on the trees. They were signs. Some of the signs said: Keep Out! No Entry! Mice Only!

Rebekah was sure that Mouse was up to something very strange now. When she sneaked closer to the voices, she saw just how strange. One by one, each of the kids was climbing a rope ladder up a very large tree. Mouse was the last one to get all the way up. When she looked up she saw that the ladder had led to a big tree house.

Chapter 6

Rebekah sat there for some time and waited for them to come down. She heard snippets of laughter. She heard voices back and forth. She didn't hear anyone calling down to her to come up.

As she walked home she was very upset. But she did not let herself cry. She would not. Mouse was obviously under some kind of mind control. Or maybe he had been invaded by an alien body snatcher. Either way, she was going to get her best friend back no matter what it took.

That night as she laid awake thinking about what might be going on with Mouse, she made a plan. She would evaluate Mouse for signs of being brainwashed. She knew him well so that she should be able to tell. So she made a list of three signs that she would look for.

Does Mouse have one of his mice?

Does Mouse have a new magic trick?

Does Mouse remember their secret handshake?

She fell asleep sure that she would be able to reveal the truth.

Chapter 7

The next day as soon as she got to school she started looking for Mouse. He wasn't easy to find. He wasn't at her locker. He was at Jaden's. She waited until Jaden had gotten his books and walked away. Then she caught up with Mouse as he turned to walk toward class. He almost walked right into her. When he looked up at her, his eyes were wide.

"H-hi," he stammered.

"Hello Mouse," Rebekah replied, her eyes narrowed. She crossed her arms over her chest and stood right in front of him. "How are your little mice?"

"Fine," he gulped. A small white mouse poked his head up out of Mouse's pocket. Rebekah frowned. She was sure that if he was brain washed he wouldn't remember to bring his pet to school with him. "I have to go now," he said quickly. He hurried away from her in the hallway before she could even say another word.

Rebekah dragged her feet all the way to class. She slumped down at her desk. She pulled out her notebook and crossed off the first test.

When the bell rang she rushed out into the hallway. She ran up and down the hall looking for Mouse. She thought at first she wouldn't find him, but then she spotted him. He was standing near the water fountain. He was whispering to Amanda. Rebekah was not shy about walking right up to Mouse this time. Amanda smiled at her as she walked past. Rebekah glared. She looked right at Mouse.

"So Mouse, do you know any knew magic tricks?" she asked, arching one eyebrow very high.

"Of course," Mouse said with a surprised smile. "Do you really want to see it?"

"Sure," Rebekah shrugged. She didn't like magic too much, but she wanted to make sure that this really Mouse and that he was in control of his own thoughts.

"Look at this," he whipped out a bright red rose. Rebekah could tell that it was not a real flower. But she played along anyway.

"Oh is that for me?" she asked.

"No, but you can smell it," he said and held it beneath her nose. Rebekah sighed and sniffed the flower. She expected it to turn into a piece of cloth, or maybe to split into two flowers. What she did not expect was a face full of water sprayed from the center of the flower.

"Mouse!" she shrieked as she wiped at her face and sputtered. "What is that? That was no magic trick!"

"Sure it is," Mouse laughed. "It's just a different kind. It's a magic trick with a joke!"

"Oh great," Rebekah said dryly. Even though she was wet she was glad that Mouse was talking to her. She fell into step beside him as they began walking to their classes.

"Mouse I really thought-"

"Rebekah, I have to go," he said quickly and ducked into his classroom. Rebekah stared after him with surprise. It was not even time for the bell to ring. She knew he didn't have to go into class that fast. Now she was really hurt. She was more than hurt. She was mad. If he didn't want to be friends with her anymore, all he had to do was say so. She marched off to her own class, fuming.

Chapter 8

As Mouse sat in his class he started to feel very bad. He knew that Rebekah probably didn't mean to hurt his feelings, even if she had. By the time school was over he decided it was time to forgive her. He waited for her outside of school. When Rebekah walked down the sidewalk, she stomped right past him as she was still upset.

"Rebekah," Mouse called out as he ran to catch up with her. "Are you doing anything this afternoon?"

"Oh just go be with your new friends," she snapped without stopping.

"Rebekah," Mouse frowned as he realized how much he must have hurt her feelings. "How about we go for ice cream, just you and me?" he said with a bright smile. Rebekah didn't want to agree. She wanted to stay mad, but she missed Mouse. He was really her best friend.

"Alright," she finally nodded. As they walked to the ice cream shop, Mouse told her about the new magic tricks that he had learned.

"So these tricks are still magic tricks, but they wind up being more like practical jokes," he laughed.

"Well if they're anything like that squirting flower, you can keep them," Rebekah said firmly.

What she really wanted to know about was the tree house she had seen in the woods. But she didn't want to upset Mouse when they were just laughing together again. She decided she would ask him about it when they went bowling the next night.

After they finished their ice cream, they both had to head home to study for the science test they had the next day. As Rebekah tried to study, she found it nearly impossible to concentrate. She really wanted to know the story behind the tree house. More importantly she wanted to know why she was not invited to be part of it.

She was still very happy that she and Mouse were talking again. As she fell asleep that night she began dreaming of the bowling alley. The only problem was, the pins were all made out of mice! Every time she rolled the ball down the alley, the mice would scatter.

Chapter 9

Rebekah woke up feeling excited the next day. She and Mouse were supposed to go bowling that night. She hurried to dress, brush her teeth, and grab her breakfast.

When she got to school she didn't see Mouse at his locker, so she just went to her own. He wasn't at lunch and this made her quite mad. She wondered if she had done something wrong. Did she order the wrong kind of ice cream? Did he know that she was rolling bowling balls at mice in her dreams?

She soon brightened up when she aced her science test. She was looking forward to sharing the news with Mouse.

When she couldn't find him after school she went to look for him by the bicycle rack. Again, he wasn't there. She was getting more and more frustrated. It was like he was avoiding her all over again. As soon as she got home she called his house.

"Hello?" Mouse answered as if nothing was the matter.

"Hello?" Rebekah replied with annoyance. "Where were you all day?"

"Oh, just a busy day," Mouse said quickly.

Rebekah frowned. She doubted that was true. "Well are you ready to go bowling tonight?" she asked.

"Oh no!" Mouse gasped. "I forgot that was tonight. I'm sorry Rebekah but I'm just too busy. I won't be able to go."

Rebekah was shocked. Mouse never missed one of their bowling nights.

"What are you busy with?" she demanded but Mouse was already hanging up the phone. "I'll find out the truth!" she insisted just before the phone cut off.

Chapter 10

When Rebekah hung up the phone, she had had enough. She was not going to let this fly. She was going to find out exactly what Mouse was up to once and for all. She grabbed her notebook, and flipped it open. There was one last test. Their secret handshake, which they hadn't used in years, but Mouse should still remember. They used it whenever they got into a fight, to show that all was forgiven.

She put her bowling ball bag back in the closet and stomped out the door. She knew just where Mouse would be, and why he was too busy. She was sure that if she got to the tree house first, the ladder would be down. But as she walked toward the park, someone zipped right in front of her. It was Amanda, with her hair streaming out behind her, riding her bike. She waved to Rebekah as she headed for the park.

Rebekah knew that if Amanda got their first she would never be able to sneak into the tree house. So she began to run, hoping to beat her somehow. As she began to run someone came flying out of a yard and on to the sidewalk. Rebekah almost ran right into Jaden.

"Oh sorry!" he said, and jogged off in the direction of the park. Now Rebekah had to catch her breath. She was getting pretty frustrated. She couldn't give up, even if she wanted to. She had to find out what was going on. Just as she reached the edge of the park she caught sight of Max running across the grassy field. Now she knew she would be too late. Her shoulders drooped as she walked across the field and into the woods. She could hear them all talking together ahead of her.

“Isn't this going to be great?” Amanda giggled.

“I can't believe it took this long,” Max replied.

"What a big surprise!" Jaden laughed.

Rebekah pouted. She wanted to know what they were talking about. She felt very left out, which made her angry and sad at the same time. All of the sudden she remembered when all of this had started. She remembered the look on Mouse's face when she didn't want to see his magic trick. This whole time she had been thinking that Mouse was the one who was being mean, but really she had started it!

"Oh no," Rebekah muttered as she realized that she had hurt Mouse's feelings. He hadn't been brainwashed, or had his body taken over by aliens, he had just been hurt. Rebekah sure knew how that felt now. She decided that if he forgave her, she would always want to see his magic tricks. Hopefully, it wasn't too late.

When she reached the tree house she was sure the ladder would already be pulled up. But instead it was dangling down against the tree. She looked up at the tree house and saw that it was dark. Maybe they hadn't gone up there? Maybe they were meeting somewhere else? Rebekah decided to check it out anyway. As she climbed up the ladder she wondered what might be inside. Just as she reached the top, lanterns turned on inside of the tree house. Rebekah peeked inside the door to find Mouse, Jaden, Max, and Amanda, huddled inside.

Chapter 11

They all smiled at her and cheered.

"Welcome to the club Rebekah," Mouse said with a wide grin.

Rebekah was very surprised. "But, I thought you didn't want me to be in it?" she said nervously.

"Rebekah if there's one thing I know, you'll always solve a mystery," Mouse laughed. "I knew you'd hunt me down tonight, so we planned a special celebration."

He pointed to the snacks and drinks covering a small table in the tree house. "All this is to welcome you to the club. That is, if you want to be in it," he added.

"Of course I do!" Rebekah said and held out her hand with her thumb folded down against her palm. He held out his hand the same way. Then they intertwined their fingers and shook twice. Then their thumbs popped out and thumb wrestled. Rebekah won!

"I'm sorry I hurt your feelings Mouse," Rebekah said with a frown.

"I know you didn't mean to," he said with a shrug. "I'm sorry I left you out. But now you can be part of Mouse's Secret Club."

"And what exactly is that?" Rebekah asked suspiciously as she crunched on a potato chip.

"You'll have to stick around to find out," he grinned and winked lightly at her. Rebekah laughed and shook her head.

"As long as you don't squirt me with any more flowers!"

"Well," Mouse grinned as he and the other kids exchanged secretive looks. "I might."

Rebekah sighed and sat down on the floor of the tree house. "Alright, tell me all about it!" she said as cheerfully as she could.

"Well, when I found this tree house I was really excited," Mouse explained as he sat down beside her. "I came up to check it out. I figured it would be full of spiders and bugs and nothing else."

"Ew," Amanda shivered.

"But there weren't any," Mouse piped up and smiled at Amanda. "In fact it was really tidy in here. Then I found this box in the corner. It was full of stuff!"

"What kind of stuff?" Rebekah asked curiously.

"Stuff like this," Jaden said as he handed her a can of peanuts.

"Tasty," Rebekah said with a grin and opened the can. A brightly colored tube sprung out at her, bopping her right in the nose. "Ugh," she sighed, as she realized it had been a trick.

"And this," Max said as he pulled out the flower that Mouse had squirted her with.

"And this," Mouse smiled proudly as he held up a book. The title read:

Magic and Mischief: A Guide to Magical Practical Jokes

"Look," Mouse said as he flipped through the pages. "It's filled with all these little notes. Someone else was using this tree house before and this book. I think it was left here for other kids to find. Some of the tricks need more than one person, so I decided to see if anyone would be interested in starting a club."

"But you didn't tell me?" Rebekah asked with a frown.

"Well, you didn't seem interested," Mouse pointed out. "And since you kind of hurt my feelings, I thought I would make the club by myself. But, the truth is, I can't have any kind of club without you being part of it Rebekah! So what do you think? Do you think you could learn to like magic?"

Rebekah thought about this for a moment. She was certainly curious.

"If it means getting to hang out with all of you, of course I can," Rebekah said with a smile.

But she whipped out her notebook. She started making notes inside. Who built the tree house? Who left the book? Mouse had his very own secret magic club, but Rebekah had a brand new mystery to solve!

Rebekah - Girl Detective #12
The Missing
Ice Cream
PJ Ryan

Rebekah - Girl Detective #12

The Missing Ice Cream

Chapter 1

As soon as Rebekah opened her eyes she was very excited. She had spent the whole night dreaming of Fudge Swirl, Cherry Garcia and Mint Chocolate Chip, all her favorite flavors of ice cream. Actually, there wasn't a flavor of ice cream that she didn't like. She would even settle for vanilla, if that was her only choice.

Rebekah hadn't been dreaming of ice cream because she went to bed early. She was dreaming of ice cream because today was the day she had been waiting for all spring. As soon as it was the official first day of summer, Mr. Sprool opened up the Ice Cream Shoppe and revealed to the whole town the brand new flavor he had created.

The flavor would only be around for the summer and Rebekah made it her job to be the very first one to taste it every year. So, as soon as the sun was up, her eyes were open and she was jumping out of bed.

She knew that Mouse would be doing the same thing. Each year they had a race to get to the Ice Cream Shoppe first. It was open all year long, but it was during the summer that they always highlighted a brand new ice cream flavor. Rebekah dressed quickly and put on her favorite ice cream cone t-shirt. Then she pulled on her shoes and raced into the kitchen. Her mother, who already knew what day it was, stood there with a banana and a glass of orange juice.

"No ice cream before breakfast Rebekah," her mother said firmly.

"But Mom," Rebekah started to complain. When her mother narrowed her eyes, Rebekah nodded quickly. "Okay, looks great, thanks!" she took the banana and the orange juice. She peeled the banana quickly, tossed the skin into the compost pile, and then scarfed it down. She followed it up with big swallows of her orange juice.

"Ugh, Rebekah you're going to make yourself sick," her mother shook her head with dismay.

"I can't help it," Rebekah giggled. "I can't wait to see what the new flavor is."

"Maybe it'll be orange banana," her mother teased with a smile.

"Nope, that was two years ago!" Rebekah reminded her.

"Oh that's right," her mother laughed. "Just be careful going into town, okay?"

"I will," Rebekah promised her. As she left the house she was glad she had something in her belly, because she was so excited that it was flipping and flopping.

Chapter 2

As Rebekah hurried down the sidewalk, she heard footsteps behind her. She knew whose they were before she even turned around.

"Mouse!" she said with a raised eyebrow.

"Rebekah," he replied with his hands on his hips.

"I guess no one wins this time," she laughed. "Why don't we just walk together?"

"Sounds good," Mouse nodded and they began to walk together toward the Ice Cream Shoppe. Their small town didn't have very much traffic, but they were still careful. When they reached the Ice Cream Shoppe, Rebekah saw Mr. Sprool flipping over the sign that hung in the glass door from closed to open.

"Hurry Mouse, before anyone else notices!" Rebekah said and began to run down the sidewalk. Mouse caught up with her just as she swung the door open. When Rebekah glanced over her shoulder at him, she noticed a small boy sitting at the corner of the shop. He had his head down and looked as if he might be taking a nap. Rebekah thought it was a little strange but she was too excited about the ice cream to pay too much attention.

"Hi Mr. Sprool!" Rebekah announced happily as she walked right up to the counter. It was high and silver, always cold to the touch. It came right to her shoulder, so she had to stand on her toes to peer over it and see the assortment of ice cream assembled in the cooler beneath. "I'm so excited to try the new flavor. What is it this year?" she asked, her eyes shining. "I do hope it has something to do with cherries and chocolate," she grinned.

Mouse nodded eagerly as he pushed his pet mouse gently back down in his front pocket. Mr. Sprool was not fond of Mouse bringing his pets into his store. “Or maybe something with peanut butter?” he asked hopefully.

"Hi Rebekah, hi Mouse," Mr. Sprool said quietly as he wiped a cloth along the other side of the counter. "I'm sorry but I'm afraid there's no new flavor this year."

"What?" Rebekah stared at him in absolute shock. "But that's not possible. You put out a new flavor every summer. Today's the day. What happened?"

He sighed and pushed his glasses up along his nose as he peered at Rebekah. He was an older man, in his eighties, and had owned the Ice Cream Shoppe for many years. He knew the parents of all the kids in the neighborhood from when they were kids themselves.

"I know you're disappointed Rebekah," he said with a slow shake of his head. "But there's nothing I can do about it. I whipped up the new flavor last night. I stuck it in the freezer and locked up. When I got here this morning to put it out, it was gone."

"Gone?" Rebekah repeated in a whisper.

"Stolen I suppose," he sighed heavily again. "It makes me so sad. Who would steal ice cream? I know I could make another new flavor, but until I find out who took the first, I'm not going to. I can't afford to waste supplies, and I had made this flavor very special," he frowned. "I guess I'm just a little upset about it."

"Of course you are," Rebekah shook her head slowly. "It is terrible that someone would steal the ice cream."

“Really terrible,” Mouse agreed as he hung his head. It was very disappointing to wait all year for something, and then find out it wasn't going to happen.

"Would you like one of the old flavors?" Mr. Sprool suggested kindly. "I'm having a special on vanilla."

"Vanilla?" Rebekah sighed and shook her head. After having so many delicious flavors of ice cream she could barely think about plain old vanilla. "No thanks Mr. Sprool. In fact, I don't want any ice cream. I'm going to save my money because I am going to have a serving of your new flavor when I figure out who took it!" she said with determination.

"Now Rebekah," Mr. Sprool warned her with a steady gaze. "Someone broke in here and stole the ice cream. That someone is a criminal. You need to be very careful when you are dealing with a criminal."

"Oh I will be," Rebekah said with confidence. "By this time tomorrow Mr. Sprool, you will have your ice cream back. Do you mind if I look in the back room where the ice cream was stored?" she asked hopefully.

"Alright, but don't disturb the sprinkles," he said with a half-smile. "If anyone can solve this mystery, I'm sure it's you, Rebekah."

Chapter 3

She smiled proudly and began walking behind the counter. Mouse started to follow her but Mr. Sprool stopped him.

"Not so fast young man," he said with a gleam in his eye. "Don't think I didn't see that you have one of your rodents in your pocket. You'll have to take that thing out of my store. For all I know it could have been animals that got into the freezer."

"But it wasn't my mouse," Mouse said with a frown.

"Maybe not," Mr. Sprool said patiently. "But mice of any kind don't belong near ice cream. Okay?"

Mouse nodded sullenly. "Yes sir," he said and waved to Rebekah. "I'll take him home and meet you back here in a little bit."

"Okay Mouse," Rebekah smiled at him. "Don't worry, I'll have this solved in no time!"

Rebekah opened the door to the back room and paid close attention to everything she saw. She had never been there before. There were lots of bowls and mixers. Large boxes of sprinkles and other toppings lined the shelves. There was also one tall freezer. This was where Mr. Sprool said the ice cream had been. When she tugged on the handle of the freezer, it was very hard to open, which meant it had been closed tight.

"Not much chance an animal could have gotten this open," she said thoughtfully as she peered inside of the freezer. The shelves were coated with a layer of frost and ice. She could see where someone had scraped across the frost.

"Hmm," she said as she looked closely at a shape that was pushed into the frost. She whipped out her notebook and drew the shape on paper. It was a diamond shape. Then she closed the freezer and looked at the floor. She could see that there was some dirt on the floor. Mr. Sprool always kept his store very clean, so she had to guess that the dirt came from the thief. As she looked closely at the dirt she saw that it was arranged into neat little lines. Like the grooves on the bottom of a shoe. She looked at the bottom of her shoe. The grooves didn't match the pattern.

"Mr. Sprool," she called out. "Could you come here for a moment," she asked.

"Sure," he stepped into the backroom.

"Can I see your shoe?" she asked.

"My shoe?" he frowned but nodded and lifted his foot into the air. He swung his arms to keep his balance as Rebekah investigated the pattern on his shoe.

"Hm, doesn't look the same," she said as she abruptly let go of his foot. Mr. Sprool steadied himself and then peered at the dirt Rebekah was looking at on the floor.

"Well that's odd," he said quietly.

"I know," Rebekah tapped her pen lightly against her chin. "Mr. Sprool, I'm getting closer to the truth."

"Good," Mr. Sprool laughed a little. "I'll leave you to it."

Chapter 4

As he opened the door to step out of the back room, Rebekah noticed the back door swung open slightly. Her eyes widened because the door had been closed and locked a moment before. She walked over to it and looked at it very closely. When she tried to turn the knob, it wouldn't budge, but the door did swing inward very easily.

"Oh no," she whispered. The door was locked alright, but it had never been closed all the way. She crouched down and looked in the groove of the door. What she found was a large pebble that had been wedged into the door frame.

"So Mr. Sprool thought everything was locked up tight last night, but it wasn't," she said with a small smile. "This is how the thief got in!"

She was sure she was getting closer to the criminal, but the question still remained. Who had committed the unspeakable crime of stealing the newest ice cream flavor?

She pushed the door open and peered into the alley behind the store. It was empty aside from a big green dumpster. She didn't see anything strange, but she did notice a trail of dirt from the recent rainstorm. She crouched down to look at it closely. It was ordinary dirt with small pebbles mixed in.

As she reached the end of the trail she noticed that there were was a shoe print in the dirt. A shoe print with the same grooves as the pattern that she had seen inside the store.

"The thief definitely came this way," she said in a whisper. As she stepped outside of the alley and on to the sidewalk, she looked in both directions. There weren't too many people on the sidewalk. But she did notice a man waiting at the bus stop. She recognized him as one of the men who worked in the grocery store.

"Mr. Green?" she asked as she walked up to him.

"Yes," he smiled at her. "Hi Rebekah, how are you doing today?"

"Not so great," she frowned. "The Ice Cream Shoppe had its newest flavor of ice cream stolen."

"Oh no," he frowned. "That's terrible."

"I know," Rebekah agreed. "I was wondering if you'd seen anyone walking in and out of that alley," she pointed at the alley behind the store.

"Uh, well," he rubbed his chin for a moment as he thought about it. "Come to think of it, I did notice someone there yesterday. He was a small man, very short. He was standing at the end of the alley for a little while and then I saw him looking in the window of the ice cream shop. Then he disappeared down the alley."

"Could you tell me anything else about how he looked?" Rebekah asked as she noted in her notebook that the suspect was short.

"I didn't see his face," Mr. Green shook his head. "Then the bus came, so I had to go. I never saw him come out of the alley."

"Hm," Rebekah said as she heard the rumbling of the bus approaching. "Thanks Mr. Green."

"No problem Rebekah, I hope you solve your mystery!"

Chapter 5

Rebekah decided to walk down the sidewalk and around behind the stores that lined it. As she walked, she thought about the clues she had found so far. She knew that the person who had stolen the ice cream was short, that they had sneaked into the back of the shop through the alley and that they had something on their hands or wrist that had the shape of a diamond. She couldn't even begin to think of what that might be.

As she reached the end of the stores she looked up at the bright lights shining over the last store in the row. It was a dollar store that sold lots of novelty toys and items for very cheap prices. She peered inside the window out of curiosity. She saw they had some new magnetic travel games as well as some new race cars on the shelf. Then she noticed that there was a new display of jewelry. Rebekah knew she was on the job, but she wanted to take a quick peek. As she stepped into the store the woman behind the counter was looking through a magazine.

"Oh wow, a customer!" she said with a happy smile. "First one of the day!"

"Hi," Rebekah smiled at the woman. She didn't know her name, but she was always very friendly. "I just wanted to look at the new jewelry."

"Oh yes, it's been very popular," the woman said as she pointed to the display. "But it's not just jewelry, there are some watches in there too. I've already sold two of them and just got the products yesterday!"

"Wow," Rebekah looked at the watches and smiled. They were very unique. Each watch face had a different shape. One was a triangle, one was a square.

"Are these all the shapes they come in?" Rebekah asked curiously.

"No, they're just the ones I have left," the woman said. "I was just about to place an order for some more of the circle and diamond shaped watches. Those are the two I already sold."

"A diamond shape?" Rebekah asked with surprise. She pulled out her notebook and flipped it open. "Does it look something like this?" she asked, her eyes wide.

"Yes actually," the woman nodded. "Just about the same."

"Wow," Rebekah cleared her throat and began taking notes in her notebook. "Do you remember who bought this watch?" she asked.

"Yes," she nodded a little. "I remember because it was a young boy. He thought about his purchase for a long time. He had one dollar and kept rolling it up and unrolling it, as if he wasn't sure if he should spend it."

"Hm," Rebekah jotted down that a young boy had bought the watch. "Did he have his mother or father with him?" Rebekah asked.

"Actually no," the woman shook her head. "I've seen him in here a few times. He is always by himself. He doesn't usually buy much, only one toy, or sometimes he only looks."

"Do you have any idea what his name might be, or where he might live?" Rebekah asked with her eyebrows raised.

"Well I did watch him walk away the first time he was here. I was a little worried about a young boy being by himself, so I poked my head out to see if his parents were waiting for him outside."

"Were they?" Rebekah made another note on her pad.

"No, so I watched the boy walk down the hill. He went into the apartment building at the end of the street," the woman explained. "Are you looking for him for some reason?"

"Well, I'm investigating some stolen ice cream," Rebekah explained.

"What?" the woman said with surprise. "Who would steal ice cream?"

"That's what I'm trying to find out," Rebekah said with a determined frown. "Thanks for all of your help!"

"You're welcome," the woman smiled.

Chapter 6

Rebekah hurried out of the shop. She ran all the way to the end of the street. The apartments were very nice, with a playground and a pool. Rebekah loved to spend time with her friends who lived there because there was always somewhere new to explore or someone new to meet.

As she headed into the apartment complex she wondered how she would figure out which apartment this boy lived in. She still couldn't believe that a young boy would be behind the missing ice cream, but she had to follow the clues.

Just then she noticed footprints on the walkway toward the apartments. They were just like the footprints she had seen in the alley. She followed them all the way to one of the apartment buildings. They stopped at the stairs.

She climbed the stairs slowly, keeping her eyes peeled for any sign of a young boy. When she reached the second story she noticed that there was a different kind of trail. A trail of drips and drops of pinkish purple ice cream. She began to follow the drips until she reached one of the apartments.

Sitting in front of the apartment, with his back to Rebekah was a young boy. He had a container on the floor in front of him and a spoon in his hand. A hand with a diamond watch on its wrist.

This had to be the thief. All the clues were there. The dirty shoes, the ice cream container, the diamond watch. It made her sad to think it could be true, but the ice cream thief was a young boy. Rebekah folded her arms across her stomach and narrowed her eyes. She stared hard at the young boy who was devouring every last bite of the delicious new ice cream flavor.

"Just what do you think you're doing Mister?" She asked sharply as she walked up behind him. The young boy froze knowing that he was caught. His ice cream spoon hung in midair with a big dollop of the tastiest looking ice cream that Rebekah had ever seen.

"Put down the spoon and turn around," Rebekah said sternly. The young boy slowly lowered the spoon but before he laid it all the way down the ice cream on it began to melt and drip on to the floor beside him. There was nothing more terrible than seeing ice cream being wasted especially the brand new flavor.

"Oh just eat it," Rebekah sighed with frustration. "Hurry before it hits the floor," she insisted. The boy gulped down the ice cream that was on the spoon. Then he turned guiltily to look at her. It was the boy she had seen sitting outside the Ice Cream Shoppe earlier in the day. His hair was now very mussed and his lips and cheeks were covered with streaks of sticky ice cream.

"So it was you," Rebekah said coolly as she studied him. "Of all the people I suspected, I never thought it would be another kid. Sure, the grown-ups did, but me, never. Because I knew that all kids hold ice cream sacred, and no one would ever hog it all for themselves," she clucked her tongue at the young boy.

Chapter 7

"Most kids," the boy said with sadness in his eyes. "Would get a chance to taste it."

"What do you mean?" Rebekah asked him as she stepped closer to him.

"I mean, every year I watch all of the other kids in town get to taste the new flavor of ice cream," he sighed as he shook his head. "Everyone but me."

"Why not you?" Rebekah asked with confusion.

"I don't have any money to buy ice cream," he frowned and kicked the empty bucket of ice cream away from him. "This year, I saved all year. I was going to make sure I got a taste of the ice cream. But when I went into the dollar store and saw the watches, I knew I really needed a watch instead.

I'm always getting home late and my mother gets upset because she worries about me. But I am always losing track of time. So I bought the watch," he frowned. "But then I was really sad because I wasn't going to get any ice cream. So yes, I stole the ice cream, and yes, I ate every last bite. I never would have had the chance to taste it if I didn't."

Rebekah was stunned by his words. She had never met anyone who didn't have enough money to buy just one serving of ice cream.

"I'm sorry," she said as she shook her head. "But all you had to do was ask."

"You mean beg?" he shot back. "No way," he crossed his arms stiffly.

"Asking isn't the same as begging silly," Rebekah frowned and picked up the empty bucket of ice cream. "But stealing is wrong no matter how you look at it."

The boy nodded his head a little and stared at the empty bucket. "I know. I just wanted to try it so badly. I was watching through the window when he made it. I saw him add in all of the ingredients and I knew it was going to be the best flavor ever.

When he left for the night, a rock got stuck in the door and it didn't close all the way. He didn't notice I guess. I was just going to go in and have a look. I wanted to see what it was like. But once I was inside, I thought how nice it would be to have my very own bucket of ice cream."

"Well you're going to have to tell Mr. Sprool the truth," Rebekah insisted and pointed down the street toward the Ice Cream Shoppe.

"Alright, alright," he hung his head as he stood up.

"What's your name anyway?" Rebekah asked as they walked toward the Ice Cream Shoppe.

"Marcus," he said with a frown.

"Well Marcus just tell Mr. Sprool the truth and tell him you're sorry. Hopefully you won't get into too much trouble." She wasn't sure about that. Marcus had stolen an entire bucket of ice cream after all.

Chapter 8

When they reached the Ice Cream Shoppe, Mr. Sprool was just about to close up for the day. He saw Rebekah and the young boy so he opened the store back up.

"Hi Rebekah," he said with a smile. "Who's your friend?"

Marcus shifted from one foot to the other. He was a little scared.

"Hi Mr. Sprool," he said sadly. "I'm sorry, but I took a bucket of ice cream from your store."

"You did?" Mr. Sprool asked with surprise. He looked closely at the young boy. "Why would you do something so terrible?"

"I just wanted to try some," Marcus frowned. "I never get to try the new flavor."

Mr. Sprool scratched his head and looked sternly at the boy. "Well now no one will get to try it, because I lost my recipe for the new flavor. If you had just asked me, I would have let you try it."

"That's what I said," Rebekah pointed out.

"I'm really sorry," Marcus stared at the ground. "I didn't think it would cause that much trouble."

"Stealing always has consequences young man," Mr. Sprool said with a wag of his finger. "I hope this is the last time you do it."

"It will be," Marcus promised and looked up at Mr. Sprool again. "I think maybe I could help, if you would let me."

"Help how?" Mr. Sprool asked curiously.

"I watched through the window when you made the new flavor and saw everything you put in it. Maybe I could help you make a new batch," he said hopefully.

"You mean I might get to taste the new flavor after all?" Rebekah asked cheerfully.

"Okay," Mr. Sproool nodded. "Let's give it a shot."

Chapter 9

While Mr. Sprool and Marcus were working on the new flavor, Rebekah ran down the street and back into her neighborhood. She ran all the way to Mouse's house. Her legs were burning she was running so fast. Breathlessly she pounded on his front door.

"Rebekah?" he asked with confusion as he opened the door. "What is it? What's going on?"

"We just might get to taste the new flavor after all!" she said happily. "Hurry up and bring Neopolitan, you know how much he likes the cheesecake flavor. We can let him eat it outside."

"Okay," Mouse ran up the stairs to grab his pet and like a bolt of lightning he was back down the stairs. "Oh I can't wait to taste that new ice cream," he nearly squealed as he and Rebekah began running back toward the Ice Cream Shoppe.

"I found the ice cream thief!" she announced between gasps for air as they ran. "Now he and Mr. Sprool are making a new batch!"

They both skidded to a stop at the corner of the road and looked to make sure no cars were coming in either direction.

"What? How did that happen?" Mouse asked with confusion.

"Try to keep up Mouse," she sighed and then explained who the thief was, and why he had stolen the ice cream and how he had offered to help Mr. Sprool make more. Once they were sure it was safe, they hurried across the street.

"I never would have thought that a kid would steal the ice cream," Mouse said with surprise. "But at least you solved the mystery!"

Chapter 10

As Rebekah flung the door of the ice cream shop open Marcus and Mr. Sprool were just stepping out into the main area of the store.

"Well?" Rebekah asked. She was out of breath and her cheeks were red from running so fast.

"We did it!" Mr. Sprool said with a broad smile. "Ready to taste?" he grinned eagerly at the three children.

"Yes we are!" Mouse said happily as he whipped out his special spoon. It was a spoon that he reserved only for tasting the newest flavor on the first day of summer. Mr. Sprool set out three cups of ice cream on the metal counter.

"Thank you," Rebekah said as she picked up her cup and laid down her dollar.

"Thank you," Mouse said as he picked up his cup and laid down his dollar.

Marcus stood perfectly still staring at the last cup of ice cream. "I don't have any money," he said with a frown.

"That's okay Marcus," Mr. Sprool said and handed him the cup. "From now on, when I introduce a new flavor, everyone gets one free cup. No one should have to go without a cup of ice cream in the summer!"

"Thanks!" Marcus said with a smile and picked up the cup.

"Are you sure you can eat more?" Rebekah laughed as she quirked a brow at him.

"Once you taste it, you'll understand," Marcus said with a confident nod. He rubbed his stomach as if it was the most delicious thing he had ever tasted.

"Let's do it!" Mouse said as he slid his spoon into the ice cream. It was a strange pinkish purple color, a color of ice cream that Rebekah had never seen before. It had little brown flecks inside of it also. She thought she spotted something blue and squishy mixed in. It smelled very sweet, with a hint of chocolate. She took a small bite of the ice cream and let it melt on her tongue.

"Oh yummy," she sighed happily. "I taste raspberry, brownie and blueberry!"

"That's right!" Mr. Sprool said with a laugh. "You get it right every year Rebekah. "It is Raspberry Blueberry Brownie Bonanza!"

"I think it's delicious," Rebekah said as she took another bite.

"Me too," Marcus said proudly. "I'm glad I had the chance to make it."

Mouse couldn't say a word. His mouth was too full.

"I'm really glad that from now on everyone will have a chance to taste the new flavor," Rebekah added as she finished her ice cream.

"And from now on I'll just ask, instead of taking what I want," Marcus said with a shy smile.

Next Steps

This book is part of the children's series, "Rebekah - Girl Detective".

I'd really love to hear from you!

I very much appreciate your reviews and comments so thank you in advance for taking a moment to leave one for "Rebekah - Girl Detective: Books 9-12."

You can join Rebekah's fun Facebook page for young detectives here:

http://www.facebook.com/RebekahGirlDetective

Sincerely,
PJ

All Titles by PJ Ryan Can be Found Here (Author Page)
http://www.amazon.com/author/pjryan

Look for the following series with more coming soon!

Rebekah – Girl Detective

RJ – Boy Detective

Mouse's Secret Club

This is a work of fiction. The characters, incidents and locations portrayed in this book and the names herein are fictitious. Any similarity to or identification with the locations, names, characters or history of any person, product or entity is entirely coincidental and unintentional.

CPSIA information can be obtained
at www.ICGtesting.com
Printed in the USA
FSHW022255011220
76502FS

9 780615 906447